Letters to Young Lovers

D1025227

Ellen G. White

Pacific Press Publishing Association
Boise, Idaho
Oshawa, Ontario, Canada

Cover Photo: D. Tank

ISBN 0-8163-0528-5

88 89 90 91 92 ● 6 5 4 3 2 1

CONTENTS

Foreword   5

I Love You   7

SECTION ONE   10
  Marriage—a Foretaste of Heaven

SECTION TWO   18
  Finding the Right Mate

SECTION THREE   28
  Is It Really Love?

SECTION FOUR   38
  Looking for Help?

SECTION FIVE   50
  In Control

SECTION SIX   62
  Sexual Responsibility

SECTION SEVEN   78
  Shadow Over the Nest

Geneva, Switzerland Dec. 16. 1885

Dear Friend   I understand that you
have desiered to have my judgment in
regard to matters that trouble you in reference
to marriage with Bro. Si   daughter
That I understand that the father of brother
the one upon whom you have placed your
affections, is not willing that his daughter
should connect with you in marriage.
While I would feel due sympathy for you because of your disappointment, I would say
that also should feel interested in his own
child more than her own father, and also
her mother. The very fact of your urgency of
this matter against the wishes of the parents
is evedence that the spirit of God has not the
first place in your heart and a controling
power upon your life. You have a strong
will a firm persistent determination to carry
out anything you have entered upon. Will my
brother please look to his own spirit and
criticise his motives, and see if he has a
single eye in this matter to act in all things

for the future immortal life.
With love to your self I remain your sister in

FOREWORD

Have you ever wondered what it would be like to receive a letter from a prophet? Would you have the courage to open the envelope and read its contents?

Throughout this book are letters written under the inspiration of God and addressed to young people to help them make the right choices relating to their courtship and marriage.

Some background material relating to the circumstances and persons involved has been introduced by the compilers. This appears on a page preceding each letter. Some lengthy letters have been abridged without deletion marks indicated; names have been changed. Additional counsels, some taken from letters, have been included in the various chapters.

At no time in life is the right kind of counsel so important as when two young people are contemplating marriage. Since the Lord loves you and wants you to have eternal life *and* a happy home, perhaps the reading of just one of these letters will help you to have *both*.

We invite you to "open the envelope" and read what the Lord has said to others like yourself.

ELLEN G. WHITE ESTATE
Washington, DC 20012

I LOVE YOU

"I LOVE YOU!" How special are those words between two young people! But even more wonderful they become when spoken to us by our Saviour who wants us to be happy and find joy in our relationship with each other.

Christ has compared His love for the church to the love of husband and wife. The Scriptures contain tender love stories such as that of Jacob and Rachel, and the moving story of Ruth, the Moabite, who through her marriage to Boaz became a link in the genealogy of the Messiah.

Our heavenly Father is concerned over our love-life. Through the inspired writings of Scripture and of Ellen G. White, God has given counsels to young people in their quest for happiness.

FROM THE BIBLE

"Behold, what manner of love the Father hath bestowed upon us, that we should be called the sons of God" (1 John 3:1).

"I am come that they might have life, and might have it more abundantly" (John 10:10).

"These things have I spoken unto you, that my joy might remain in you, and that your joy might be full" (John 15:11).

"He that toucheth you toucheth the apple of his eye" (Zechariah 2:8).

"This love of which I speak is slow to lose patience—it looks for a way of being constructive. It is not possessive: it is neither anxious to impress nor does it cherish inflated ideas of its own importance.

"Love has good manners and does not pursue selfish advantage. It is not touchy. It does not keep account of evil or gloat over the wickedness of other people. On the contrary, it is glad with all good men when truth prevails.

"Love knows no limit to its endurance, no end to its trust, no fading of its hope; it can outlast anything. It is, in fact, the one thing that still stands when all else has fallen" (1 Corinthians 13: 4-8 Phillips).

"The Lord hath appeared of old unto me, saying, Yea, I have loved thee with an everlasting love; therefore with loving-kindness have I drawn thee" (Jeremiah 31:3).

"For I am persuaded, that neither death, nor life, nor angels, nor principalities, nor powers, nor things present, nor things to come,

"Nor height, nor depth, nor any other creature, shall be able to separate us from the love of God, which is in Christ Jesus our Lord" (Romans 8:38, 39).

FROM THE WRITINGS OF ELLEN G. WHITE

I write because I love your soul.—*Letter 51, 1889.*

Dear youth, I wish to speak decidedly to you, because I want you to be saved.—*Messages to Young People,* p. 140.

My dear sister, I have written to you because I have a love for your soul.—*Letter 51,* 1894.

I do not consider your case hopeless; if I did my pen would not be tracing these lines.—*Testimonies,* vol. 2, p. 562.

Take reproof as from God, take counsel and advice given in love.—*Letter 30,* 1875.

Keep your wants, your joys, your sorrows, your cares, and your fears before God. You cannot burden Him; you cannot weary Him. He who numbers the hairs of your head is not indifferent to the wants of His children. "The Lord is very pitiful, and of tender mercy." James 5:11. His heart of love is touched by our sorrows and even by our utterances of them. Take to Him everything that perplexes the mind. Nothing is too great for Him to bear, for He holds up worlds, He rules over all the affairs of the universe. Nothing that in any way concerns our peace is too small for Him to notice. There is no chapter in our experience too dark for Him to read; there is no perplexity too difficult for Him to unravel. No calamity can befall the least of His children, no anxiety harass the soul, no joy cheer, no sincere prayer escape the lips, of which our heavenly Father is unobservant, or in which He takes no immediate interest. "He healeth the broken in heart, and bindeth up their wounds." Psalm 147:3. The relations between God and each soul are as distinct and full as though there were not another soul upon the earth to share His watchcare, nor another soul for whom He gave His beloved Son.—*Steps to Christ,* p. 100.

SECTION ONE

Marriage—a Foretaste of Heaven

The warmth of true friendship and the love that binds the hearts of husband and wife are a foretaste of heaven.

God has ordained that there should be perfect love and perfect harmony between those who enter into the marriage relation.

Let bride and bridegroom in the presence of the heavenly universe pledge themselves to love one another as God has ordained they should.—
In Heavenly Places, p. 202.

A FORETASTE OF HEAVEN

Man was not made to dwell in solitude; he was to be a social being. Without companionship the beautiful scenes and delightful employments of Eden would have failed to yield perfect happiness. Even communion with angels could not have satisfied his desire for sympathy and companionship. There was none of the same nature to love and to be loved.

God Himself gave Adam a companion. He provided "an help meet for him"—a helper corresponding to him—one who was fitted to be his companion, and who could be one with him in love and sympathy. Eve was created from a rib taken from the side of Adam, signifying that she was not to control him as the head, nor to be trampled under his feet as an inferior, but to stand by his side as an equal, to be loved and protected by him. A part of man, bone of his bone, and flesh of his flesh, she was his second self, showing the close union and the affectionate attachment that should exist in this relation. "For no man ever yet hated his own flesh; but nourisheth and cherisheth it." Ephesians 5:29. "Therefore shall a man leave his father and his mother, and shall cleave unto his wife; and they shall be one."

God celebrated the first marriage. Thus the institution has for its originator the Creator of the universe. "Marriage is honor-

11

able'' (Hebrews 13:4); it was one of the first gifts of God to man, and it is one of the two institutions that, after the Fall, Adam brought with him beyond the gates of Paradise. When the divine principles are recognized and obeyed in this relation, marriage is a blessing; it guards the purity and happiness of the race, it provides for man's social needs, it elevates the physical, the intellectual, and the moral nature.[1]

As the Creator joined the hands of the holy pair [Adam and Eve] in wedlock, saying, A man shall ''leave his father and his mother and shall cleave unto his wife; and they shall be one'' (Genesis 2:24), He enunciated for all the children of Adam.

That which the Eternal Father Himself had pronounced good was the law of highest blessing and development for man.''[2]

MAKE YOUR COURTSHIP LAST
THROUGHOUT YOUR MARRIAGE

Not one word should be spoken, not one action performed, that you would not be willing the holy angels should look upon and register in the books above. You should have an eye single to the glory of God. The heart should have only pure, sanctified affection, worthy of the followers of Jesus Christ, exalted in its nature, and more heavenly than earthly. Anything different from this is debasing, degrading in courtship; and marriage cannot be holy and honorable in the sight of a pure and holy God, unless it is after the exalted Scriptural principle.

Let some of the hours of courtship before marriage run through the married life.[3]

"EXCEPT THE LORD BUILD
THE HOUSE" Psalm 127:1

Those who are contemplating marriage should consider what will be the character and influence of the home they are founding. As they become parents, a sacred trust is committed to them. Upon them depends in a great measure the well-being of their children in this world, and their happiness in the world to come. To a great extent they determine both the physical and moral stamp that the little ones receive. And upon the character of the home depends the condition of society; the weight of each family's influence will tell in the upward or the downward scale.

The choice of a life companion should be such as best to secure physical, mental, and spiritual well-being for parents and for their children—such as will enable both parents and children to bless their fellow men and to honor their Creator.[4]

Jesus did not begin His ministry by some great work before the Sanhedrin at Jerusalem. At a household gathering in a little Galilean village His power was put forth to add to the joy of a wedding feast. Thus He showed His sympathy with men, and His desire to minister to their happiness.[5]

He who gave Eve to Adam as a helpmeet, performed His first miracle at a marriage festival. In the festal hall where friends and kindred rejoiced together, Christ began His public ministry. Thus He sanctioned marriage, recognizing it as an institution that He Himself had established.[6]

The presence of Christ alone can make men and women happy. All the common waters of life Christ can turn into the wine of heaven. The home then becomes as an Eden of bliss; the family, a beautiful symbol of the family in heaven.[7]

Edson was the second of Ellen White's four sons. Because of her extensive travel and other responsibilities throughout her busy life, she had to be away from her children. A large collection of her letters to them has been preserved. The following letter was written to Edson and Emma in 1870 shortly after their marriage, and represents a mother's hopes and prayers for the home that has just been established. The counsel shows a loving mother's care for her son, but carries the added dimension of her own experience in receiving divine messages from the Lord in visions.

September, 1870

Dear Edson and Emma:

You, my children, have given your hearts to one another; unitedly give them wholly, unreservedly to God. In your married life seek to elevate one another. Show the high and elevating principles of your holy faith in your everyday conversations and in the most private walks of life. Be ever careful and tender of the feelings of one another. Do not allow a playful, bantering, joking censuring of one another. These things are dangerous. They wound. The wound may be concealed, nevertheless the wound exists and peace is being sacrificed and happiness endangered.

My son, guard yourself and in no case manifest the least disposition savoring of a dictatorial, overbearing spirit. It will pay to watch your words before speaking. This is easier than to take them back or efface their impression afterward. Ever speak kindly. Modulate even the tones of your voice. Let only love, gentleness, and mildness be expressed in your countenance and in your voice. Make it a business to shed rays of sunlight, but never leave a cloud. Emma will be all to you you can desire if you are watchful and give her no occasion to feel distressed and troubled and to doubt the genuineness of your love. You yourselves can make your happiness or lose it. You can by seeking to conform your life to the Word of God be true, noble, elevated, and smooth the pathway of life for each other.

Yield to each other. Edson, yield your judgment sometimes. Do not be persistent, even if your course appears just right to yourself. You must be yielding, forbearing, kind, tenderhearted, pitiful, courteous, ever keeping fresh the little courtesies of life, the tender acts, the tender, cheerful, encouraging words. And may the best of heaven's blessings rest upon you both, my dear children, is the prayer of your mother.

Mother

Letter 24, 1870

MARRIAGE IS LIKE CHRIST'S LOVE
FOR HIS CHOSEN PEOPLE

In both the Old and the New Testament the marriage relation is employed to represent the tender and sacred union that exists between Christ and His people, the redeemed ones whom He has purchased at the cost of Calvary.

"Fear not," He says; "thy Maker is thine husband; the Lord of hosts is His name, and thy Redeemer, the Holy One of Israel." "Turn, O backsliding children, saith the Lord; for I am married unto you." Isaiah 54:4, 5; Jeremiah 3:14. In the "Song of Songs" we hear the bride's voice saying, "My Beloved is mine, and I am His." And He who is to her "the chiefest among ten thousand," speaks to His chosen one. "Thou art all fair, My love; there is no spot in thee." Song of Solomon 2:16; 5:10; 4:7.[8]

MARRIED LIFE GETS BETTER AND BETTER

Men and women can reach God's ideal for them if they will take Christ as their helper. What human wisdom cannot do, His grace will accomplish for those who give themselves to Him in loving trust. His providences can unite hearts in bonds that are of heavenly origin. Love will not be a mere exchange of soft and flattering words. The loom of heaven weaves with warp and woof finer, yet more firm, than can be woven by the looms of earth. The result is not a tissue fabric, but a texture that will bear wear and test and trial. Heart will be bound to heart in the golden bonds of a love that is enduring.[9]

To love as Christ loved means to manifest unselfishness at all times and in all places, by kind words and pleasant looks. These cost those who give them nothing, but they leave behind a fragrance that surrounds the soul. Their effect can

16

never be estimated. Not only are they a blessing to the receiver, but to the giver; for they react upon him. Genuine love is a precious attribute of heavenly origin, which increases in fragrance in proportion as it is dispensed to others.

Christ's love is deep and earnest, flowing like an irrepressible stream to all who will accept it. There is no selfishness in His love. In this heaven-born love is an abiding principle in the heart, it will make itself known, not only to those we hold most dear in sacred relationship, but to all with whom we come in contact. It will lead us to bestow little acts of attention, to make concessions, to perform deeds of kindness, to speak tender, true, encouraging words. It will lead us to sympathize with those whose hearts hunger for sympathy.[10]

2—L.Y.L.

SECTION TWO
Finding the Right Mate

BE PRACTICAL

Before assuming the responsibilities involved in marriage, young men and young women should have such an experience in practical life as will prepare them for its duties and its burdens.[1]

Since both men and women have a part in homemaking, boys as well as girls should gain a knowledge of household duties. To make a bed and put a room in order, to wash dishes, to prepare a meal, to wash and repair his own clothing, is a training that need not make any boy less manly; it will make him happier and more useful.[2]

There are very many girls who have married and have families, who have but little practical knowledge of the duties devolving upon a wife and mother. They can read, and play upon an instrument of music; but they cannot cook. They cannot make good bread, which is very essential to the health of the family. They can-

not cut and make garments, for they never learned how. They considered these things unessential, and in their married life they are as dependent upon some one to do these things for them as are their own little children.[3]

WHAT A YOUNG MAN SHOULD
LOOK FOR IN A WIFE

Let a young man seek one to stand by his side who is fitted to bear her share of life's burdens, one whose influence will ennoble and refine him, and who will make him happy in her love.[4]

"A prudent wife is from the Lord." "The heart of her husband doth safely trust in her." "She will do him good and not evil all the days of her life." "She openeth her mouth with wisdom; and in her tongue is the law of kindness. She looketh well to the ways of her household, and eateth not the bread of idleness. Her children arise up, and call her blessed; her husband also, and he praiseth her. Many daughters have done virtuously, but thou excellest them all." "Whoso findeth a wife findeth a good thing, and obtaineth favour of the Lord." Proverbs 19:14; 31:11, 12, 26-29; 18:22.

Rolf was the son of a leading minister in Europe. The girl he wanted to marry was not sure if she loved him, but he was urging her to make a commitment to him.

There were other problems that indicate she was not ready to take on the responsibilities of married life, either by temperament or by training. Ellen White asks some questions of Rolf that should be answered by every young man who plans for marriage.

Dear Rolf:

While at Basel I had some conversation with Edith in regard to your attentions to her. I asked her if her mind was fully made up that she loves you well enough to link her interests with you for life. She answered that she was not fully settled upon this point. I told her that she should know just what steps she was taking; that she should give no encouragement to the attentions of any young man showing him preference unless she loved him.

She plainly stated that she did not know as she did love you, but thought if she were engaged to you she might become acquainted with you. But as it was you both had no opportunity to become acquainted.

I had reason to think that she disliked domestic labor, and I knew that you should have a wife that could make you a happy home. I asked her if she had any experience in those duties that make a home. She answered that she had done housework at home in her father's family. I asked these questions because as her character had been presented to me she needed special education in practical duties of life, but had no taste or inclination for these things.

She told me that she was not decided in anything, that you were very urgent and loved her, but she could not say that she loved you although you were very kind and attentive. Said I, "Then come to an understanding. Do not lead him on."

I told her she should consider the object of a marriage with you, whether by such a step you could both glorify God; whether you would be more spiritual; and whether your lives would be more useful. Marriages that are impulsive and selfishly planned generally do not result well but often turn out miserable failures.

Now, Rolf, I cannot say that it is my business to say that you shall not marry Edith, but I will say that I have an interest in you. Here are things which should be considered: Will the one *you marry bring happiness to your home? Is Edith an economist, or will she if married not only use up all her own earnings, but all of yours to gratify a vanity, a love of appearance? Are her principles correct in this direction?*

I do not think Edith knows what self-denial is. If she had the opportunity she would find ways to spend even more means than she has done. With her, selfish gratifications have never been overcome, and this natural self-indulgence has become a part of her life. She desires an easy, pleasant time.

I must speak plainly. I know, Rolf, that should you marry her you would be mated, but not matched. There would be something wanting in the one you make your wife. And as far as Christian devotion and piety is concerned, that can never grow where so great selfishness possesses the soul.

I will write to you, Rolf, just as I would write to my son. There is a great and noble work lying just before us, and the part we shall act in this world depends wholly upon our aims and purposes in life. We may be following impulse. You have the qualities in you to make a useful man, but if you follow inclination, this strong current of self-will will sweep you away. Place for yourself a high standard, and earnestly strive to reach it.

Let it become the ruling purpose of your heart to grow to a complete man in Christ Jesus. In Christ you can do valiantly; without Christ you can do nothing as you should. You have a determination to carry out that which you purpose. This is not an objectionable feature in your character if all your powers are surrendered to God. Please bear this in mind, that you are not at liberty to dispose of yourself as your fancy may dictate. Christ has purchased you with a price that is infinite. You are His property, and in all your plans you must take this into account.

Especially in your marriage relations, be careful to get one who will stand shoulder to shoulder with you in spiritual growth.

Rolf, I want you to consider all these things. God help you to pray over this matter. Angels are watching this struggle. I leave you with this matter to consider and decide for yourself.

Letter 23, 1886   *Ellen G. White,*

QUESTIONS A GIRL SHOULD
ASK BEFORE MARRIAGE

Before giving her hand in marriage, every woman should inquire whether he with whom she is about to unite her destiny is worthy. What has been his past record? Is his life pure? Is the love which he expresses of a noble, elevated character, or is it a mere emotional fondness? Has he the traits of character that will make her happy? Can she find true peace and joy in his affection? Will she be allowed to preserve her individuality, or must her judgment and conscience be surrendered to the control of her husband? As a disciple of Christ, she is not her own; she has been bought with a price. Can she honor the Saviour's claims as supreme? Will body and soul, thoughts and purposes, be preserved pure and holy? These questions have a vital bearing upon the well-being of every woman who enters the marriage relation.[5]

Let the questions be raised, Will this union help me heavenward? will it increase my love for God? and will it enlarge my sphere of usefulness in this life? If these reflections present no drawback, then in the fear of God move forward.

True love is a plant that needs culture. Let the woman who desires a peaceful, happy union, who would escape future misery and sorrow, inquire before she yields her affections, Has my lover a mother? What is the stamp of her character? Does he recognize his obligations to her? Is he mindful of her wishes and happiness? If he does not respect and honor his mother, will he manifest respect and love, kindness and attention, toward his wife? When the novelty of marriage is over, will he love me still? Will he be patient with my mistakes, or will he be critical, overbearing, and dictatorial? True affection will overlook many mistakes; love will not discern them.[6]

Let a young woman accept as a life companion only one who possesses pure, manly traits of character, one who is diligent, aspiring and honest, one who loves and fears God.[7]

This letter to Nellie looks at some of the same questions as the earlier one to Rolf. The crowd she is associating with is not good. Her special friend is irreverent, lazy, and uses foul language as well. Other habits are questionable also. Ellen White asks some very straightforward questions that might well apply to you as you read this letter.

Dear Nellie:

I am thankful to God that you love the truth, that you love Jesus, and I am anxious that you should press your way forward and upward in order that you shall reach the standard of Christian character that is revealed in the word of God. Let the word of God be your guidebook that in everything you may be molded in conduct and character according to its requirements.

You are the Lord's property both by creation and redemption. You may be a light in your home, and may continually exercise a saving influence in living out the truth. When the truth is in the heart its saving influence will be felt by all that are in the house. A sacred responsibility is resting upon you, and one that requires that you keep your soul pure by consecrating yourself to be wholly the Lord's.

Your acquaintances who are utterly averse to spiritual things, are not refined, ennobled, and elevated by the practice of the truth. They are not under the leadership of Christ, but under the black banner of the prince of darkness. To associate with those who neither fear nor love God—unless you associate with them for the purpose of winning them to Jesus—will be a detriment to your spirituality. If you cannot lift them up, their influence will tell upon you in corrupting and tainting your faith. It is right for you to treat them kindly, but not well for you to love and choose their society; for if you choose the atmosphere that surrounds their souls, you will forfeit the companionship of Jesus.

From the light which the Lord has been pleased to give me, I warn you that you are in danger of being deceived by the enemy. You are in danger of choosing your own way and of not following the counsel of God and not walking in obedience to His will. The Holy One has given rules for the guidance of every soul so that no one need miss his way. These directions mean everything to us, for they form the standard to which every son and daughter of Adam should conform.

You are just entering upon womanhood, and if you seek the grace of Christ, if you follow the path where Jesus leads the way, you will become more and more a true woman. You will grow in grace, become wiser by experience, and as you advance from light to a greater light you will become happier. Remember your life belongs to Jesus, and that you are not to live for yourself alone.

Shun those who are irreverent. Shun one who is a lover of idleness; shun the one who is a scoffer of hallowed things. Avoid the society of one who uses profane language or is addicted to the use of even one glass of liquor. Listen not to the proposals of a man who has no realization of his responsibility to God. The pure truth which sanctifies the soul will give you courage to cut yourself loose from the most pleasing acquaintance whom you know does not love and fear God, and knows nothing of the principles of true righteousness. We may always bear with a friend's infirmities and with his ignorance, but never with his vices.

Be cautious every step that you advance; you need Jesus at every step. Your life is too precious a thing to be treated as of little worth. Calvary testifies to you of the value of your soul. Consult the word of God in order that you may know how you should use the life that has been purchased for you at infinite cost. As a child of God you are permitted to contract marriage only in the Lord. Be sure that you do not follow the imagination of your own heart, but move in the fear of God.

If believers associate with unbelievers for the purpose of winning them to Christ, they will be witnesses for Christ, and having fulfilled their mission, will withdraw themselves in order to breathe in a pure and holy atmosphere. When in the society of unbelievers, ever remember that in character you are a representative of Jesus Christ, and let no light and trifling words, no cheap conversation be upon your lips.

Keep in mind the value of the soul, and remember that it is your privilege and your duty to be in every possible way a laborer together with God. You are not to lower yourself to the same level as that of unbelievers, and laugh and make the same cheap speeches.

The Lord will be your helper, and if you trust Him, will bring you up to a noble, elevated standard, and will place your feet upon the platform of eternal truth. Through the grace of Christ you can make a right use of your entrusted capabilities and become an agent for good in winning souls to Christ. Every talent you have should be used on the right side.

My dear sister, I have written to you because I have a love for your soul, and I beseech you to hear my words. I have more to write to you when I shall find time.

With Christian love,

Ellen G. White,

SECTION THREE

Is It Really Love?

He [Satan] is busily engaged in influencing those who are wholly unsuited to each other to unite their interests. He exults in this work, for by it he can produce more misery and hopeless woe to the human family than by exercising his skill in any other direction.[1]

Many marriages can only be productive of misery; and yet the minds of the youth run in this channel because Satan leads them there, making them believe that they must be married in order to be happy, when they have not the ability to control themselves or support a family. Those who are not willing to adapt themselves to each other's disposition, so as to avoid unpleasant differences and contentions, should not take the step.[2]

This question of marriage should be a study instead of a matter of impulse.[3]

IS IT TRUE LOVE?

True love is a high and holy principle, altogether different in character from that love which is awakened by impulse and which suddenly dies when severely tested.[4]

True love is not a strong, fiery, impetuous passion. On the contrary, it is calm and deep in its nature. It looks beyond mere externals and is attracted by qualities alone. It is wise and discriminating, and its devotion is real and abiding.[5]

Love is a precious gift, which we receive from Jesus. Pure and holy affection is not a feeling, but a principle. Those who are actuated by true love are neither unreasonable nor blind.[6]

Mildness, gentleness, forbearance, long-suffering, being not easily provoked, bearing all things, hoping all things, enduring all things—these are the fruit growing upon the precious tree of love, which is of heavenly growth. This tree, if nourished, will prove to be an evergreen. Its branches will not decay, its leaves will not wither. It is immortal, eternal, watered continually by the dews of heaven.[7]

LOVE, A TENDER PLANT

Love is a plant of heavenly growth, and it must be fostered and nourished. Affectionate hearts, truthful, loving words, will make happy families and exert an elevating influence upon all who come within the sphere of their influence.[8]

While women want men of strong and noble characters, whom they can respect and love, these qualities need to be mingled with tenderness and affection, patience and forbearance. The wife should in her turn be cheerful, kind, and devoted, assimilating her taste to that of her husband as far as it is possible to do without losing her individuality. Both parties should cultivate patience and kindness, and that tender love for each other that will make married life pleasant and enjoyable.

Those who have such high ideas of the married life, whose imagination has wrought out an air-castle picture that has naught to do with life's perplexities and troubles, will find themselves sadly disappointed in the reality. When real life comes in with its troubles and cares, they are wholly unprepared to meet them. They expect in each other perfection, but find weakness and defects; for finite men and women are not faultless. Then they begin to find fault with each other, and to express their disappointment. Instead of this, they should try to help each other, and should seek practical godliness to help them to fight the battle of life valiantly.[9]

THE POWER OF LOVE

LOVE is power. Intellectual and moral strength are involved in this principle, and cannot be separated from it. The power of

wealth has a tendency to corrupt and destroy; the power of force is strong to do hurt; but the excellence and value of pure love consist in its efficiency to do good, and to do nothing else than good.

WHATSOEVER is done out of pure love, be it ever so little or contemptible in the sight of men, is wholly fruitful; for God regards more with how much love one worketh than the amount he doeth.

LOVE is of God. The unconverted heart cannot originate nor produce this plant of heavenly growth, which lives and flourishes only where Christ reigns. . . .

LOVE works not for profit nor reward; yet God has ordained that great gain shall be the certain result of every labor of love. It is diffusive in its nature and quiet in its operation, yet strong and mighty in its purpose to overcome great evils. It is melting and transforming in its influence, and will take hold of the lives of the sinful and affect their hearts when every other means has proved unsuccessful.

WHEREVER the power of intellect, of authority, or of force is employed, and love is not manifestly present, the affections and will of those whom we seek to reach assume a defensive, repelling position, and their strength of resistance is increased.

PURE LOVE is simple in its operations, and is distinct from any other principle of action. The love of influence and the desire for the esteem of others may produce a well-ordered life and frequently a blameless conversation. Self-respect may lead us to avoid the appearance of evil. A selfish heart may perform generous actions, acknowledge the present truth, and express humility and affection in an outward manner, yet the motives may be deceptive and impure; the actions that flow from such a heart may be destitute of the savor of life and the fruits of true holiness, being destitute of the principles of pure love.

LOVE should be cherished and cultivated, for its influence is divine.[10]

WHEN LOVE IS BLIND

Two persons become acquainted; they are infatuated with each other, and their whole attention is absorbed. Reason is blinded, and judgment is overthrown. They will not submit to any advice or control, but insist on having their own way, regardless of consequence.

Like some epidemic, or contagion, that must run its course, is the infatuation that possesses them; and there seems to be no such thing as putting a stop to it. Perhaps there are those around them who realize that, should the parties interested be united in marriage, it could only result in life-long unhappiness. But entreaties and exhortations are given in vain. Perhaps, by such a union, the usefulness of one whom God would bless in His service will be crippled and destroyed; but reasoning and persuasion are alike unheeded.

All that can be said by men and women of experience proves ineffectual; it is powerless to change the decision to which their desires have led them. They lose interest in everything that pertains to religion. They are wholly infatuated with each other, and

33

the duties of life are neglected, as if they were matters of little concern.

The good name of honor is sacrificed under the spell of this infatuation, and the marriage of such persons cannot be solemnized under the approval of God. They are married because passion moved them, and when the novelty of the affair is over, they will begin to realize what they have done. In six months after the vows are spoken, their sentiments toward each other have undergone a change. Each has learned in married life more of the character of the companion chosen. Each discovers imperfections that, during the blindness and folly of their former association were not apparent. The promises at the altar do not bind them together. In consequence of hasty marriages, even among the professed people of God, there are separations, divorces, and great confusion in the church.

When it is too late, they find that they have made a mistake, and have imperiled their happiness in this life and the salvation of their souls. They would not admit that any one knew anything about the matter but themselves, when if counsel had been received, they might have saved themselves years of anxiety and sorrow.

34

But advice is only thrown away on those who are determined to have their own way. Passion carries such individuals over every barrier that reason and judgment can interpose.[11]

Weigh every sentiment, and watch every development of character in the one with whom you think to link your life destiny. The step you are about to take is one of the most important in your life, and should not be taken hastily. While you may love, do not love blindly.[12]

I hope you will have self-respect enough to shun this form of courtship. If you have an eye single to the glory of God, you will move with deliberate caution. You will not suffer lovesick sentimentalism to so blind your vision that you cannot discern the high claims that God has upon you as a Christian.[13]

Several challenging questions are raised in this letter. It seems that both are too young and immature to consider marriage. Some evidences of immaturity are suggested. There is the problem of superficiality on the part of the girl. The question of whether it is real love or infatuation is considered. Ellen White urges this young man to take the long look rather than to think only of the moment.

Dear John:

I am sorry that you have entangled yourself in any courtship with Elizabeth. In the first place, your anxiety upon this question is premature.

I speak to you as one who knows. Wait till you have some just knowledge of yourself and of the world, of the bearing and character of young women, before you let the subject of marriage possess your thoughts.

Elizabeth will never elevate you. She has not in her the hidden powers which, developed, would make a woman of judgment and ability to stand by your side, to help you in the battles of life. She lacks force of character. She has not depth of thought and compass of mind that will be a help to you. You see the surface and it is all there is. In a little while, should you marry, the charm would be broken. The novelty of the married life having ceased, you will see things in their real light, and find out you have made a sad mistake.

Love is a sentiment so sacred that but few know what it is. It is a term used, but not understood. The warm glow of impulse, the fascination of one young person for another is not love; it does not deserve the name. True love has an intellectual basis, a deep thorough knowledge of the object loved.

Remember that impulsive love is perfectly blind. It will as soon be placed on unworthy objects as worthy. Command such love to stand still and cool. Give place to genuine thought and deep, earnest reflection. Is this object of your affection, in the scale of intelligence and moral excellence, in deportment and cultivated manners such that you will feel a pride in presenting her to your father's family, to acknowledge her in all society as the object of your choice?

Give yourself sufficient time for observation on every point, and then do not trust to your own judgment, and let the mother who loves you, and your father, and confidential friends, make critical observations of the one you feel inclined to favor. Trust not to your own judgment, and marry no one whom you feel will not be an honor to your father and mother, one who has intelligence and moral worth.

The girl who gives over her affections to a man, and invites his attention by her advances, hanging around where she will be noticed of him, unless he shall appear rude, is not the girl you want to associate with. Her conversation is cheap and frequently without depth.

It will be far better not to marry at all, than to be unfortunately married. But seek counsel of God in all these things, be so calm, so submissive to the will of God that you will not be in a fever of excitement and unqualified for His service by your attachments.

We have but little time to lay up a treasure of good works in heaven; do not make any mistake here. Serve God with your undivided affection. Be zealous, be whole-hearted. Let your example be of such a character that you will help others to take their stand for Jesus. Young men do not know what a power of influence they may have. Work for time and work for eternity.

Your adopted mother,

Ellen G. White,

SECTION FOUR

Looking for Help?

HAVE I MADE THE RIGHT CHOICE?

We are not to place the responsibility of our duty upon others, and wait for them to tell us what to do. We cannot depend for counsel upon humanity. The Lord will teach us our duty just as willingly as He will teach somebody else. If we come to Him in faith, He will speak His mysteries to us personally. Our hearts will often burn within us as One draws nigh to commune with us as He did with Enoch. Those who decide to do nothing in any line that will displease God, will know, after presenting their case before Him, just what course to pursue. And they will receive not only wisdom, but strength. Power for obedience, for service, will be imparted to them as Christ has promised.[1]

Marriage is something that will influence and affect your life both in this world and in the world to come. A sincere Christian will not advance his plans in this direction without the knowledge that God approves his course. He will not want to choose for Himself, but will feel that God must choose for him. We are not to please ourselves, for Christ pleased not Himself. I would not be understood to mean that anyone is to marry one whom he does not love. This would be sin. But fancy and the emotional nature must not be allowed to lead on to ruin. God requires the whole heart, the supreme affections.[2]

If men and women are in the habit of praying twice a day before they contemplate marriage, they should pray four times a day when such a step is anticipated. Marriage is something that will influence and affect your life, both in this world and in the world to come. A sincere Christian will not advance his plans in this direction without the knowledge that God approves his course.[3]

If there is any subject that should be considered with calm reason and unimpassioned judgment, it is the subject of marriage. If ever the Bible is needed as a counselor, it is before taking a step that binds persons together for life.[4]

Instituted by God, marriage is a sacred ordinance and should never be entered upon in a spirit of selfishness. Those who contemplate this step should solemnly and prayerfully consider its importance and seek divine counsel that they may know whether they are pursuing a course in harmony with the will of God. The instruction given in God's word on this point should be carefully considered. Heaven looks with pleasure upon a marriage formed with an earnest desire to conform to the directions given in the Scripture.[5]

Belle does not seem to want counsel from any source—even from those closest to her, and most interested in her happiness. Ellen White suggests that she ought to listen to her parents, and in turn is disappointed that her own counsel has been ignored. She pleads that if Belle is unwilling to go to human help, she should certainly turn to God. Here are two letters Mrs. White wrote to her.

Dear Belle:

I hoped to meet you and talk with you. I greatly fear that you disregard the light which the Lord has been pleased to give you through me. I know that the Lord has tender, pitying love toward you, and I hope you will not under temptation be led to pursue a course to separate your soul from God. There are many who are ready to give advice and confuse the mind with counsel, who have not God for their counselor, therefore all they may say will only make a mixed case of one that is already very trying.

Belle, your disposition and temperament is such that I greatly fear for your soul. I fear that you will not choose for your companions those who are discreet and wise and humble in heart, who love God and who keep His commandments.

Abstain from even the appearance of evil, is the exhortation of the inspired apostle. Have you done this? The sensational and emotional is more fully developed than the intellectual. Everything, Belle, should be avoided that would exaggerate this tendency into a predominating power. You have motive power; let it be uncorrupted and wholly devoted to God. God has bestowed upon you capabilities and powers to be sanctified and exercised to His glory.

You have a history and you are making history. The mind may in this crisis of your life take a turn, a bias of grossness rather than of refinement. The contaminating influences of the world may mold your habits, your taste, your conversation, your deportment. You are on the losing side. The precious moments, so solemn, fraught with eternal results, may be wholly on Satan's side of the question and may prove your ruin. I do not want it thus. I want you should be a Christian, a child of God, an heir of heaven.

You are in danger of giving up Christ, of becoming reckless and unwilling to listen to wise counsel. The counsel of parental affection is lost upon deaf ears. Will you, Belle, think seriously whether you will receive advice from the experienced? Will you be guided by your friends? Will the parental counsel be unheeded? Will you take your case in your own hands?

I hope you will change your course of action, for if the Lord has ever spoken by me, He now speaks to you to retrace your steps. Your passions are strong, your principles are endangered, and you will not consider and will not follow advice which you know to be good and the only clear, safe, consistent thing for you to do. Will you resolve to do right, to be right, to heed the counsel I have given you in the name of the Lord? God has given you capabilities. Shall they be wasted at random? Unguided efforts will go more often in the wrong direction than the right. Will you let years of waywardness, disappointment, and shame pass and you make so many wrong impressions on minds by your course of action that you can never have that influence which you might have had?

In order to gain that which you think is liberty you pursue a course which, if followed, will hold you in a bondage worse than slavery. You must change your course of conduct and be guided by the counsel of experience and through the wisdom of those whom the Lord teaches, place your will on the side of the will of God.

But if you are determined to listen to no counsels, but your own and you will work out every problem for yourself, then be sure you will reap that which you have sown. You will miss the right way altogether or else, wounded, bruised, and dwarfed in religious character, you will turn to the Lord, humbled, penitent, and confessing your errors. You will become tired of beating the air.

Remember every action and every course of action has a two-fold character, be it virtuous or demoralizing. God is displeased with you. Can you afford to pursue the course you are pursuing?

Ellen G. White

Letter 47, 1889

Letter No. 2

Dear Belle:

Again my heart goes out to you. How is it with your soul? Have you a conscience void of offense toward God and man? Your associations, are they of that character to draw your mind to God and to heavenly things, to increase in you reverence for your parents, pure and holy aspirations? Do you love the truth and the right? Or are you indulging in a creative imagination that has no healthful influence upon the soul? Can you look back upon the last year of your life with satisfaction? Can you see a growth in spiritual power? Any low gratification, any self-indulgence, is a scar left upon the soul, and the noble powers of mind are corrupted. There may be repentance, but the soul is crippled, and will wear its scars through all time. Jesus can wash away the sin but the soul has sustained a loss.

I beg of you, Belle, to go to God for wisdom. The most difficult thing you will have to manage is your own self. Your own daily trials, your emotions, and your peculiar temperament, your inward promptings,–these are difficult matters for you to control, and these wayward inclinations bring you often into bondage and darkness.

Your only course is to give yourself unreservedly into the hands of Jesus–all your experiences, all your temptations, all your trials, all your impulses–and let the Lord mold you as clay is molded in the hands of the potter. You are not your own and therefore there is the necessity of giving your unmanageable self into the hands of One who is able to manage you. Then rest, precious rest and peace will come to your soul.

Belle, it is not now too late for wrongs to be righted. It is not now too late to make your calling and your election sure. You may now begin to work upon the plan of addition. Add to your faith virtue, and knowledge, and temperance, and patience, and every Christian grace. Everything else will perish in the great day of conflagration, but the gold of holy character is enduring. It knows no decay. It will stand the test of the fires of the last day. My dear child, I wish you to remember that "God shall bring every work into judgment, with every secret thing, whether it be good, or whether it be evil." Ecc. 12:14.

What are you doing, Belle? Have you, since you decided to discard counsel, to refuse advice, been growing into a firm, well developed Christian? Or have you, in choosing your own way, found it brings unrest, cares, and worries?

Why not listen to the advice of your parents? Before you is the path that leads to certain ruin. Will you turn while you can? Will you seek the Lord while Mercy's sweet voice is appealing to you, or will you still have your own way? The Lord pities you. The Lord invites you. Will you come?

May the Lord help you to choose to be wholly the Lord's. I write because I love your soul.

Ellen G. White,

Letter 51, 1889

PARENTS CAN BE OF HELP

If you are blessed with God-fearing parents, seek counsel of them. Open to them your hopes and plans; learn the lessons which their life experiences have taught.[6]

Should a son or daughter select a companion without first consulting the parents, when such a step must materially affect the happiness of parents if they have any affection for their children? And should that child, notwithstanding the counsel and entreaties of his parents, persist in following his own course? I answer decidedly: No; not if he never marries. "Honor thy father and thy mother: that thy days may be long upon the land which the Lord thy God giveth thee." Here is a commandment with a promise which the Lord will surely fulfill to those who obey. Wise parents will never select companions for their children without respect to their wishes.[7]

One of the greatest errors connected with this subject is that the young and inexperienced must not have their affections disturbed, that there must be no interference in their love experience. If there ever was a subject that needed to be viewed from every standpoint, it is this. The aid of the experience of others, and a calm, careful weighing of the matter on both sides, is positively essential. It is a subject that is treated altogether too lightly by the great majority of people. Take God and your God-fearing parents into your counsel, young friends. Pray over the matter.

If children would be more familiar with their parents, if they would confide in them, and unburden to them their joys and sorrows, they would save themselves many a future heartache. When perplexed to know what course is right, let them lay the matter just as they view it before their parents and ask advice of them. Who are so well calculated to point out their dangers as godly parents? Who can understand their peculiar temperaments so well as they? Children who are Christians will esteem above every earthly blessing the love and approbation of their God-fearing parents. The parents can sympathize with the children, and pray for and with them that God will shield and guide them.[8]

This letter brings into focus the thought of responsibility to parents. It is clear that Hans is trying to urge himself upon the girl, against the strong opposition of her parents, and without concern for their feelings at all. This situation raises the question of whether parents should be considered in the process of choosing a wife. What happens after such a marriage as far as relations with them are concerned? Ellen White poses such consequences worth considering.

Dear Hans:

I understand that you have desired to have my judgment in regard to matters that trouble you in reference to marriage with Brother Meyer's daughter. I understand that the father of the one upon whom you have placed your affections is not willing that his daughter should connect with you in marriage. While I would feel due sympathy for you because of your disappointment, I would say, "Who should feel interested in his own child more than her own father; and also her mother?"

The very fact of your urgency of this matter against the wishes of the parents is evidence that the Spirit of God has not the first place in your heart and a controlling power upon your life. You have a strong will, a firm, persistent determination to carry out anything you have entered upon.

Will my brother please look to his own spirit and criticize his motives and see if he has a single eye in this matter to act in all things for the glory of God? I was shown the cases of several in Switzerland who were very much exercised upon the subject of marriage, that they had their minds so fully engrossed with this subject that they were disqualifying themselves to do the work God would have them to do.

There was a young man shown me who was seeking to become one of the family of Brother Meyer's whom he did not seem to accept. He was in great trial and worriment of mind. I cannot but think this applies to you. This brother was not fitted in any sense to take the responsibilities of a husband or of a family, and should the union be formed now there would be great unhappiness as the result.

Now, my brother, my advice is for you to give your mind and affections to God and lay yourself on the altar of God.

There is the fifth commandment that must be respected. Had this commandment been more respected than it has been,—had children been obedient to their parents and thus honored them,— how much suffering and misery would have been spared! The inexperienced child cannot discern what is for her best good, and how to wisely choose a companion who will make her life pleasant and happy; and an unhappy marriage is the greatest calamity that can befall both parties.

Will my brother closely examine his heart and see whether he is in the love of God or not? Will he see what feelings are arising there against Brother Meyer because he cannot bring his mind to consent to there being a union between you and his daughter? If you were indeed learning in the school of Christ to wear His yoke, to lift His burdens, to learn of Jesus' meekness and lowliness of heart, you would not urge your will and your wishes so persistently.

Do not unfit yourself through your strong will to carry your points at all hazards. Stop where you are and inquire, "What is the spirit that controls me?" Are you loving God with all your heart? Are you loving your neighbor as yourself?

The very first duty that rests upon Brother Meyer's daughter is to obey her parents, to honor her father and her mother. This she can do if you will not keep her mind in a state so unsettled that she cannot do her duty to her parents.

The mother needs the help of her child, and when she will become a few years older, she will understand better how to choose a husband who will make her life smooth and happy. A woman who will submit to be ever dictated to in the smallest matters of domestic life, who will yield up her identity, will never be of much use or blessing in the world and will not answer the purpose of God in her existence. She is a mere machine, to be guided by another's will and another's mind. God has given each one, men and women, an identity, an individuality. All must act in the fear of God for themselves.

There are so many unhappy marriages. Can we be surprised that parents are cautious and want to guard their children from any connection which may not be wise and best?

Your sister in Christ

Ellen G. White,

Letter 25, 1885

DON'T KEEP IT A SECRET

A young man who enjoys the society and wins the friendship of a young lady unbeknown to her parents, does not act a noble Christian part toward her or toward her parents. Through secret communications and meetings he may gain an influence over her mind; but in so doing he fails to manifest that nobility and integrity of soul which every child of God will possess. In order to accomplish their ends, they act a part that is not frank and open and according to the Bible standard, and prove themselves untrue to those who love them and try to be faithful guardians over them. Marriages contracted under such influences are not according to the word of God. He who would lead a daughter away from duty, who would confuse her ideas of God's plain and positive commands to obey and honor her parents, is not one who would be true to the marriage obligations.

"Thou shalt not steal" was written by the finger of God upon the tables of stone; yet how much underhand stealing of affections is practiced and excused. A deceptive courtship is maintained, private communications are kept up, until the affections of one who is inexperienced, and knows not whereunto these things may grow, are in a measure withdrawn from her parents and placed upon him who shows by the very course he pursues that he is unworthy of her love. The Bible condemns every species of dishonesty, and demands right doing under all circumstances.[9]

SECTION FIVE

In Control

POWER IN CHRIST FOR SELF-CONTROL

All are accountable for their actions while in this world upon probation. All have power to control their actions if they will. If they are weak in virtue and purity of thoughts and acts, they can obtain help from the Friend of the helpless. Jesus is acquainted with all the weaknesses of human nature, and, if intreated, will give strength to overcome the most powerful temptations. All can obtain this strength if they seek for it in humility.[1]

"Whether therefore ye eat, or drink, or whatsoever ye do, do all to the glory of God." [1 Cor. 10:31] Here is a principle which lies at the foundation of every act, thought, and motive; the consecration of the entire being, both physical and mental, to the control of the Spirit of God. . . . You can do all things through Christ, who strengtheneth you.[2]

BEFORE YOU SAY "I DO!"

Early marriages are not to be encouraged. A relation so important as marriage and so far-reaching in its results should not be entered upon hastily, without sufficient preparation, and before the mental and physical powers are well developed.[3]

Attachments formed in childhood have often resulted in very wretched unions, or in disgraceful separations. Early connections, if formed without the consent of parents, have seldom proved happy. . . . After their judgment has become more matured, they view themselves bound for life to each other, and per-

51

haps not at all calculated to make each other happy. Then, instead of making the best of their lot, recriminations take place, the breach widens, until there is settled indifference and neglect of each other. To them there is nothing sacred in the word "home." The very atmosphere is poisoned by unloving words and bitter reproaches.[4]

BROKEN ENGAGEMENTS

Even if an engagement has been entered into without a full understanding of the character of the one with whom you intend to unite, do not think that the engagement makes it a positive necessity for you to take upon yourself the marriage vow and link yourself for life to one whom you cannot love and respect. Be very careful how you enter into conditional engagements; but better, far better, break the engagement before marriage than separate afterward, as many do.[5]

Mary Anne seems self-centered and willful, not always exercising the best judgment in choice of friends. The young man of her special choice is from a prominent Adventist family, and yet is irreligious, making fun of the church and spiritual things. He is deceptive, putting on a front to Mary, pretending to be something he is not, in order to win her heart. Ellen White considers the almost hypnotic effect such a relationship can have, and asks some things that get right to the heart of the situation.

Dear Mary Anne:

I have been shown some things in reference to you which I dare not withhold longer because I feel you to be in danger. God loves you and He has given you unmistakable evidences of His love. Jesus has bought you with His own blood, and what have you done for Him?

You love yourself, love to enjoy pleasure, and love the society of young men; and you fail to discriminate between the worthy and the unworthy. You have not experience and judgment and are in danger of taking a course which will prove to be all wrong and result in your ruin. You have strong affections, but your inexperience would lead you to have them placed upon improper objects. You should be guarded and not follow the bent of your own mind.

We are, my dear child, living amid the perils of the last days. Satan is intent upon corrupting the minds of youth with thoughts and affections and sympathies that they think are real genuine love which must not be interfered with. This I was shown is your case. You little know how very anxious and how great burdens your parents have borne for you.

You have not honored your father and your mother as God requires of you. The sin which exists in this generation among children is that they are "disobedient to parents, unthankful, unholy, lovers of pleasure more than lovers of God." And this state of things exists to such an extent that it is made a subject of prophecy as one of the signs that we are living in the last days of time.

God has claims upon you. He has blessed you with life and with health and with capabilities and reasoning powers that you may, if you will improve, or you may greatly abuse by yielding these powers or qualities of mind to the control of Satan. You are responsible for the ability which God has given you.

You may, by making the most of your privileges, fit yourself for a position of influence and duty.

I was shown in my last vision that there are many of the young in Battle Creek who have not the fear of God before them, who are not at all religiously inclined. And there is still another class who are scoffers. Among the latter is Arthur Jones. He has all his life been rebellious. He has dishonored his father and his mother. The restraint of home and parental authority he has despised and rebelled against. He has not been subdued. A rebellious spirit is as natural as his breath. He is quarrelsome at home, disobedient, heady, highminded, unthankful and unholy. Such a spirit you are favoring. You are allowing your affections to go out after this boy. Stop just where you are. Do not allow this matter to go one step farther.

I was shown that he was a scorner of religion, a miserable unbeliever, a skeptic. He makes sport of religious things. He puts on a fair exterior to keep favor with you, but his entire life has been rebellious at home and rebellious against God.

No matter how he talks and deceives you, God looks upon him as he is, and I warn you not to cherish feelings of affection for this young man. Sever all intimate and close connection with the young man. He is unworthy of your love. He would not respect you if he will not respect and honor his parents.

You must not be ready to dispose of your heart's affections. You are young and you are unsuspecting. You will surely be deceived unless you are more guarded. God has purposes for you which Satan wishes to defeat. Give yourself unreservedly to God; connect with heaven.

Do not be led away from your Redeemer by an irreligious young man, a scorner of sacred things. Sever the intimacy existing between you at once. Do not follow your inclination, but follow your Saviour. Eternal life, my dear child, eternal life you want at any cost. Do not sacrifice this for your pleasure, to follow your own feelings, but give yourself to Jesus, love Him and live to His glory.

Take these words written, act upon them and God will bless you abundantly. Take reproof as from God, take counsel and advice given in love.

God has given you golden opportunities. Improve them. Make the most of the time you have now. Set your soul to seek God *earnestly. Humble your heart before Him and in the simplicity of humble faith, take up your cross and your responsibilities and follow the Pattern given you. Heaven will be cheap enough. The precious immortal life will be given to all who choose the path of humble obedience.*

Will you from this time, make an entire change in your life and seek to know what is the will of God concerning you? Neglect not this time of privilege, but here, right here, lay all at the feet of Jesus and serve Him with your individual affections. God help you to break off the shackles Satan has sought to bind upon you.

In haste and much love,

Ellen G. White,

Letter 30, 1875

This letter has some of the sternest warnings and counsels from the Lord's prophet found in this book. It seems that Elizabeth has so many personal problems and weaknesses that her case is hopeless. This letter at first sounds like it could be considered a final judgment from God, but right in the middle of all the rebuke are the following words of encouragement:

"I do not consider your case hopeless; if I did, my pen would not be tracing these lines." Ellen White concludes with a strong appeal for conversion of Elizabeth.

Dear Elizabeth:

I was shown that you were in danger of being under the full control of the great adversary of souls. You have been opposed to restraint, have been headstrong, willful, and stubborn, and have made your parents much trouble. They have erred. Your father has unwisely petted you. You have taken advantage of this and have become deceptive. You have received approbation which you did not deserve.

At school you had a good and noble teacher, yet you felt indignant because you were restrained. You thought that because you were the daughter of Elder Cole, your teacher should show a preference for you and should not take the liberty to correct and reprove you. While in school, you were sometimes troublesome, impudent, and defiant, and greatly lacked modesty and decorum. You were bold, selfish, and self-exalted, and needed firm discipline at home as well as at school.

You have received incorrect ideas in regard to girls' and boys' associating together, and it has been very congenial to your mind to be in the company of the boys. You have been injured by reading love stories and romances, and your mind has been fascinated by impure thoughts. Your imagination has become corrupt, until you seem to have no power to control your thoughts. Satan leads you captive as he pleases.

Your conduct has not been chaste, modest, or becoming. You have not had the fear of God before your eyes. My dear girl, unless you stop just where you are ruin is surely before you. Cease your day-dreaming, your castle-building. Stop your thoughts from running in the channel of folly and corruption.

If you indulge in vain imaginations, permitting your mind to dwell upon impure thoughts, you are, in a degree, as guilty before God as if your thoughts were carried into action. All that prevents the action is the lack of opportunity.

You will have to become a faithful sentinel over your eyes, ears, and all your senses if you would control your mind and prevent vain and corrupt thoughts from staining your soul.

The imagination must be positively and persistently controlled if the passions and affections are made subject to reason, con-

science, and character. You are in danger, for you are just upon the point of sacrificing your eternal interests at the altar of passion. Passion is obtaining positive control of your entire being—passion of what quality? of a base, destructive nature.

I appeal to you to stop where you are. Advance not another step in your headstrong, wanton course; for before you are misery and death. Unless you exercise self-control in regard to your passions and affections you will surely bring yourself into disrepute with all around you, and will bring upon your character disgrace which will last while you live.

I do not consider your case hopeless; if I did, my pen would not be tracing these lines. In the strength of God, you can redeem the past. You may even now gain a moral excellence so that your name may be associated with things pure and holy. You can be elevated. God has provided for you the necessary helps.

You have thought so much of yourself, of your own smartness, that it has led you to such affectation and vanity as to make you almost a fool. You have a deceitful tongue, which has indulged in misrepresentation and falsehood. Oh, my dear girl, if you could only arouse, if your slumbering, deadened conscience could be awakened, and you could cherish a habitual impression of the presence of God, and keep yourself subject to the control of an enlightened, wakeful conscience, you would be happy yourself and a blessing to your parents, whose hearts you now wound. You could be an instrument of righteousness to your associates. You need a thorough conversion, and without it you are in the gall of bitterness, and in the bonds of iniquity.

Put marriage out of your girl's head. You are in no sense fit for this. You need years of experience before you can be qualified to understand the duties, and take up the burdens, of married life.

You may become a prudent, modest, virtuous girl, but not without earnest effort. You must watch, you must pray, you must meditate, you must investigate your motives and your actions. Closely analyze your feelings and your acts. Would you, in the presence of your father, perform an impure action? No, indeed. But you do this in the presence of your heavenly Fa-

ther, who is so much more exalted, so holy, so pure. Yes; you corrupt your own body in the presence of the pure, sinless angels, and in the presence of Christ; and you continue to do this irrespective of conscience; irrespective of the light and warnings given you.

Yield yourself to Christ without delay; He alone, by the power of His grace, can redeem you from ruin. He alone can bring your moral and mental powers into a state of health. Your heart may be warm with the love of God; your understanding, clear and mature, your conscience, illuminated, quick, and pure; your will, upright and sanctified, subject to the control of the Spirit of God. You can make yourself what you choose. If you will now face rightabout, cease to do evil and learn to do well, then you will be happy indeed; you will be successful in the battles of life, and rise to glory and honor in the better life than this. "Choose you this day whom ye will serve."

Ellen G. White,

DON'T BE SQUEEZED
INTO THE WORLD'S MOLD

Those who would not fall a prey to Satan's devices, must guard well the avenues of the soul; they must avoid reading, seeing, or hearing that which will suggest impure thoughts. The mind must not be left to dwell at random upon every subject that the enemy of souls may suggest. The heart must be faithfully sentineled, or evils without will awaken evils within, and the soul will wander in darkness.[6]

Those who would have that wisdom which is from God must become fools in the sinful knowledge of this age, in order to be wise. They should shut their eyes, that they may see and learn no evil. They should close their ears, lest they hear that which is evil and obtain that knowledge which would stain their purity of thoughts and acts. And they should guard their tongues, lest they utter corrupt communications and guile be found in their mouths.[7]

We are commanded to crucify the flesh, with the affections and lusts. How shall we do it? Shall we inflict pain on the body? No, but put to death the temptation to sin. The corrupt thought is to be expelled. Every thought is to be brought into captivity to Jesus Christ. All animal propensities are to be subjected to the higher powers of the soul. The love of God must reign supreme; Christ must occupy an undivided throne. Our bodies are to be regarded as His purchased possession. The members of the body are to become the instruments of righteousness.[8]

PORNOGRAPHY AND YOUR MIND

Many of the young are eager for books. They read everything they can obtain. Exciting love stories and impure pictures have a corrupting influence. Novels are eagerly perused by many, and, as the result, their imagination becomes defiled. Photographs of females in a state of nudity are frequently circulated for sale.

This is an age when corruption is teeming everywhere. The lust of the eye and corrupt passions are aroused by beholding and by reading. The heart is corrupted through the imagination. The mind takes pleasure in contemplating scenes which awaken the lower and baser passions. These vile images, seen through defiled imagination, corrupt the morals and prepare the deluded, infatuated beings to give loose rein to lustful passions.

Avoid reading and seeing things which will suggest impure thoughts. Cultivate the moral and intellectual powers. Let not these noble powers become enfeebled and perverted by much reading of even storybooks.[9]

Satan has come down with great power to work his deceptions. He fastens the mind or imaginations upon impure, unlawful things. Christians become like Christ in character by dwelling upon the divine Model. That with which they come in contact has a molding influence upon life and character. I have read of a painter who would never look upon an imperfect painting for a single moment, lest it should have a deteriorating influence upon his own eye and conceptions. That which we allow ourselves to look upon oftenest, and think of most, transfers itself in a measure to us.[10]

SECTION SIX
Sexual Responsibility

SEXUAL RESPONSIBILITY OF YOUNG CHRISTIANS

The surrender of all our powers to God greatly simplifies the problem of life. It weakens and cuts short a thousand struggles with the passions of the natural heart.[1]

The young affections should be restrained until the period arrives when sufficient age and experience will make it honorable and safe to unfetter them.[2]

A little time spent in sowing your wild oats, dear young friends, will produce a crop that will embitter your whole life; an hour of thoughtlessness, once yielding to temptation, may turn the whole current of your life in the wrong direction. You can have but one youth; make that useful. When once you have passed over the ground, you can never return to rectify your mistakes. He who refuses to connect with God, and puts himself in the way of temptation will surely fall. God is testing every youth.[3]

Sensuality is the sin of the age. But the religion of Jesus Christ will hold the lines of control over every species or unlawful liberty: the moral powers will hold the lines of control over every thought, word, and action. Guile will not be found in the lips of the true Christian. Not an impure thought will be indulged in, not a word spoken that is approaching to sensuality, not an action that has the least appearance of evil.

Do not see how close you can walk upon the brink of a precipice, and be safe. Avoid the first approach to danger. The soul's interests cannot be trifled with. Your capital is your character. Cherish it as you would a golden treasure. Moral purity, self-

respect, a strong power of resistance, must be firmly and constantly cherished.[4]

Every unholy passion must be kept under the control of sanctified reason through the grace abundantly bestowed of God in every emergency. But let no arrangement be made to create an emergency, let there be no voluntary act to place one where he will be assailed with temptation, or give the least occasion for others to think him guilty of indiscretion.[5]

As long as life shall last, there is need of guarding the affections and the passions with a firm purpose. There is inward corruption, there are outward temptations, and wherever the work of God shall be advanced, Satan plans so to arrange circumstances that temptation shall come with overpowering force upon the soul. Not one moment can we be secure only as we are relying upon God, the life hid with Christ in God.[6]

William is apparently totally infatuated with Carol. In this series of letters, we see the continuing effort of Ellen White to get through to him. Carol has encouraged a friendship that has almost totally absorbed the attention of both of them. It has gone far beyond the bounds of what is right and honorable, and they are deeply involved in practices that should, as Ellen White says, be reserved for marriage.

Such a relationship threatens the future usefulness of both William and Carol. Ellen White urges that either they break it off, or get married, so they don't ruin their reputations, and effect their witness as Christians.

65

Dear William:

I go to my tent with aching heart, to relieve my mind by writing you some things which were shown me in vision.

The Lord has shown you that your association with Carol was not in any way calculated to help your morals or strengthen your spirituality. You have made some feeble attempts to break away from her society, but you have soon renewed your attention to her, she sometimes making the advance, and you infatuated with her.

You have spent hours of the night in her company because you were both infatuated. She professes love for you but she knows not the pure love of an unpretending heart.

I was shown you are fascinated, deceived, and Satan exults that one who has scarcely a trait of character that would make a happy wife and a happy home should have an influence to separate you from the mother who loves you with a changeless affection. In the name of the Lord cease your attentions to Carol or marry her–do not scandalize the cause of God.

You have pursued your own course irrespective of consequences. Your heart has rebelled against your mother because she could not in any way receive Carol or sanction the attention you gave her.

The intimacy formed with Carol has not had a tendency to bring you nearer the Lord or to sanctify you through the truth. You are risking your eternal interest in the company of this girl.

Carol expects to consummate a marriage with you and you have given her encouragement to expect this by your attentions. Your happiness in this life and in the future life is in peril. You have followed her deceptive, foolish entreaties and your own judgment which have not made you a more consistent Christian or a more faithful, dutiful son. If the atmosphere surrounding her is the most agreeable to you, if she meets your standard for a wife to stand at the head of your family; if, in your calm judgment, taken in the light given you of God, her example would be worthy of imitation, you might as well marry her as to be in her society and conduct yourselves as only man and wife should conduct themselves towards each other.

Your acts and conversation are offensive to God. The angels of God bear record of your words and your actions. The light has been given you but you have not heeded it. The course you have pursued is a reproach to the cause of God. Your behaviour is unbecoming and unchristian. When you should both be in your beds you have been in one another's society and in one another's arms nearly the entire night. Have your thoughts been more pure, more holy, more elevated and ennobled? Did you have clear views of duty—greater love for God and the truth?

Your friend,

Ellen G. White,

Dear William:

I arise early this morning. My mind is not at rest in regard to you. Your case was shown me. The Ledger of Heaven was opened and I read there a record of your life.

You cast most bitter reflection upon yourself that you had trusted to your own judgment and walked in your own wisdom, rejected the voice of God, despised the warnings and advice of His servants, and with a perseverance and persistency followed your own pernicious ways by which the way of truth was evil spoken of, and souls were lost who might have been saved through your instrumentality.

Much more I might relate in reference to you, but this is enough for the present. I felt so grateful when I came out of vision and found it was not a present reality, that probation still lingered. And now I call upon you to make haste and no longer trifle with eternal things.

You flatter yourself that you are honest, but you are not. You have been and still are welding the chains by your own course of conduct with Carol that will hold you in the veriest bondage. The voice of God you have rejected: the voice of Satan you have heeded. You act like a man bereft of his senses, and for what? A girl without principle, without one really loveable trait of character, proud, extravagant, self-willed, unconsecrated, impatient, heady, without natural affection, impulsive. Yet if you cut entirely loose she might stand a better chance to see herself and humble her heart before God.

It is always a critical period in a young man's life when he is separated from home influences and wise counsels and enters upon new scenes and trying tests. If, without will or choice of his own, he is placed in dangerous positions and relies upon God for strength—cherishing the love of God in his heart—he will be kept from yielding to temptation by the power of God who placed him in that trying position.

What a difference there was in Joseph's case and the case of young men who apparently force their way into the very field of the enemy, exposing themselves to the fierce assaults of Satan.

The Lord prospered Joseph, but in the midst of his prosperity comes the darkest adversity. The wife of his master is a licentious woman, one who urged his steps to take hold on hell. Will Joseph yield his moral gold of character to the seductions of a corrupt woman? Will he remember that the eye of God is upon him?

Few temptations are more dangerous or more fatal to young men than the temptation to sensuality, and none if yielded to will prove so decidedly ruinous to soul and body for time and eternity. The welfare of his entire future is suspended upon the decision of a moment. Joseph calmly casts his eyes to heaven for help, slips off his loose outer garment, leaving it in the hand of his tempter, and while his eye is lighted with determined resolve in the place of unholy passion, he exclaims, "How can I do this great wickedness and sin against God?" The victory is gained; he flees from the enchanter; he is saved.

You have had an opportunity to show whether your religion was a practical reality. You have taken liberties in the sight of God and holy angels that you would not take under the observation of your fellow men. True religion extends to all the thoughts of the mind, penetrating to all the secret thoughts of the heart, to all the motives of action, to the object and direction of the affections, to the whole framework of our lives. "Thou God seest me," will be the watchword, the guard of the life. You may take these lessons home. You have need to learn, and may God help you.

Ellen G. White,

Dear William:

I feel a deep interest that this last call shall not be treated indifferently as the former have been. It is the last invitation you will have, if you do not heed this.

It remains to be seen now whether you will pursue the course of infatuation you have done, whether Carol will after her confession do the same that she has done. I was shown her course was like this, she would make open acknowledgement and then draw upon your sympathies in a most pathetic manner in letters and in conversation. You have been drawn to her again to give her sympathy and encouragement and you were so weak, so completely blinded that you were entangled again more firmly than ever.

You were shown me in her society hours of the night; you know best in what manner these hours were spent. You called on me to speak whether you had broken God's commandments. I ask you, Have you not broken them? How was your time employed hours together night after night? Were your position, your attitude, your affections such that you would want them all registered in the Ledger of Heaven? I saw, I heard things that would make angels blush.

No young man should do as you have done to Carol unless married to her; and I was much surprised to see that you did not sense this matter more keenly. I write now to implore you for your soul's sake to dally with temptation no longer. Make short work in breaking this spell that like a fearful nightmare has brooded over you. Cut yourself loose now and forever, if you have any desire for the favor of God.

Such a course as you have pursued has been enough to destroy confidence in you as an honest man and as a Christian, and unless you were under the bewitching of satanic power you would not have done as you have. But I stand in doubt of you now whether you will change your course of action. I know the power that holds his enchantment over you, and I want you to see and sense it before it shall be too late. Will you now change entirely, cut the last connection with Carol? Will she do this on her part? If neither of you will do this, marry her at once and disgrace yourselves and the cause of God no more.

You have signally failed in almost every respect. Now the rest of your life seek to get back what you have lost. Let the Ledger of Heaven give a different record of your course.

God bless you.

Ellen G. White,

Dear William:

I am pleased to receive a letter from you and was pleased to read your suggestions that it was your mind to remain where you are until you have proved yourself or undone the influence you have exerted. I am pleased that you feel thus. I have, you will see, written very positively and plainly for thus the matter was shown me, and the regard I have for your soul prompted me to relate your case as it was shown me, as one of great peril. It will be difficult for you to see it thus, but in a dream last night you were saying to your mother, If this is the way the case really is, there is no use for me to try for I should fail.

Said I, William, when you try with all perseverance and determined will to retrace your steps and recover yourself from Satan's snare, you will escape from your bondage and be a free man. It will require a strong will, in the strength of Jesus, to break up the force of habit, dismiss the adversary of souls that has been entertained by you so long. Exchange guests, and welcome Jesus to take possession of the soul temple. But He does not share the heart with Satan. You can make even now in this late period a determined effort, not in your strength but in the strength of Jesus.

Let your heart break before God and confess and forsake those things which have separated you from God. This is the work of repentance that you must begin with your mother. You will never come to the light unless you do this. Leave no work undone that you can do to make wrongs right, for you have come now to the crisis.

You will have the trial, you will be proved of God. If you come forth as pure gold, then God will use you. Be not faithless, but believing. Your trial will not be for the present joyous, but rather, grievous, but it will afterwards yield the peaceable fruit of righteousness. "Whom the Lord loveth He chasteneth, and scourgeth every son whom He receiveth. If ye endure chastening, God dealeth with you as with sons; for what son is he whom the father chasteneth not?" (Hebrews 12:6, 7)

Now your steps must be down deep in the valley of humiliation. You have felt, my mountain stands sure. I can keep myself. But your past experience and your present position is one that should give you clear discernment of man's depravity because of his departure from God.

Now, my dear boy, for Christ's sake enter into no further deception in your course. Work as for eternity. Confer not with yourself, but let your heart break before God lest that stone fall upon you and grind you to powder.

What more shall I say to you? What can I say? I want you to be saved. I want you to stand perfect before God.

Yours in love,

Ellen G. White,

TRIFLING WITH HEARTS

To trifle with hearts is a crime of no small magnitude in the sight of a holy God. And yet some will show preference for young ladies and call out their affections, and then go their way and forget all about the words they have spoken and their effect. A new face attracts them, and they repeat the same words, devote to another the same attentions.

This disposition will reveal itself in the married life. The marriage relation does not always make the fickle mind firm, the wavering steadfast and true to principle. They tire of constancy, and unholy thoughts will manifest themselves in unholy actions.[7]

The women in this age, both married and unmarried, too frequently do not maintain the reserve that is necessary. They encourage the attentions of single and married men, and those who are weak in moral power will be ensnared. Thoughts are awakened that would not have been if woman had kept her place in all modesty and sobriety.

By being circumspect, reserved, taking no liberties, receiving no unwarrantable attentions, but preserving a high moral tone and becoming dignity, much evil might be avoided.[8]

Women are too often tempters. On one pretense or another they engage the attention of men, married or unmarried, and lead them on till they transgress the law of God, till their usefulness is ruined, and their souls are in jeopardy.

Shall not the women professing the truth keep strict guard over themselves, lest the least encouragement be given to unwarrantable familiarity? They may close many a door of temptation if they will observe at all times strict reserve and propriety of deportment.[9]

Janet is impulsive, and is in danger of making decisions that will affect her own life and her witness to others in a negative way. Ellen White urges her to put school first at the time, and thus prepare for a useful life for the Lord.

Janet worked for a period of time in Ellen White's home, thus they were personally acquainted with each other.

Dear Janet:

I have been awakened early this morning at three o'clock. I was in earnest conversation with you in the night, and was saying, "Janet, the Lord has a work for you to do." I was presenting before you the perils of your past life.

I have felt the burden laid upon me to have a watch-care for your soul. You are in danger of making grievous blunders in following impulse. God has saved you from entering into marriage relations with persons who were not in any way calculated to make you happy, and who were corrupt in morals and would have fastened you in Satan's snare, where you would have been miserable in this life and imperiled your soul. Will not the past lessons be sufficient for you? You are altogether too free with your affections, and would if left to your own course of action make a life-long mistake. Do not sell yourself at a cheap market.

You must take heed and not be careless of your associations. In order to act your part in the service of God, you must go forth with the advantages of as thorough an intellectual training as possible. You need a vigorous, symmetrical development of the mental capabilities, a graceful, Christian, many-sided development of culture, to be a true worker for God.

You must consider every step in the light that you are not your own, you are bought with a price. I write you this now, and will write again ere long, for as the mistake of your past life has been set before me, I dare not withhold most earnest entreaties that you hold yourself strictly to discipline.

You are now in your student's life; let your mind dwell upon spiritual subjects. Keep all sentimentalism apart from your life. You are now in the formative period of character; nothing with you is to be considered trivial or unimportant which will detract from your highest, holiest interest, your efficiency in the preparation to do the work God has assigned you.

It is your duty to remove every objectionable feature of character that you may be complete in Christ Jesus. You have a large fund of affection and will need to be constantly guarded lest you bestow your affection upon unworthy objects. Character is formed for usefulness and duty by studying the life and character of Jesus Christ, who is our Pattern.

You cannot be too careful and too particular in all your ways. Let the influence wherever you are be of that character to help and bless others. God has a work for you to do. In no case put your neck under a yoke that will be galling all your life. Be true to yourself and true to your God, and you will have the favor of God, which is of more value than life itself. I pray the Lord to bless you abundantly.

Ellen G. White,

Letter 23, 1893

SECTION SEVEN

Shadow Over the Nest

SHADOW OVER THE NEST

The heart yearns for human love, but this love is not strong enough, or pure enough, or precious enough to supply the place of the love of Jesus. Only in her Saviour can the wife find wisdom, strength, and grace to meet the cares, responsibilities, and sorrows of life. She should make Him her strength and her guide. Let woman give herself to Christ before giving herself to any earthly friend, and enter into no relation which shall conflict with this.

Those who would find true happiness must have the blessing of Heaven upon all that they possess and all that they do. It is disobedience to God that fills so many hearts and homes with misery. My sister, unless you would have a home where the shadows are never lifted, do not unite yourself with one who is an enemy of God.

To connect with an unbeliever is to place yourself on Satan's ground. You grieve the Spirit of God and forfeit His protection. Can you afford to have such terrible odds against you in fighting the battle for everlasting life?[1]

"If two of you shall agree on earth as touching any thing that they shall ask, it shall be done for them of My Father which is in heaven." But how strange the sight! While one of those so closely united is engaged in devotion, the other is indifferent and careless; while one is seeking the way to everlasting life, the other is in the broad road to death.[2]

CAN TWO WALK TOGETHER
EXCEPT THEY BE AGREED?

I have been shown the cases of some who profess to believe the truth, who have made a great mistake by marrying unbelievers. The hope was cherished by them that the unbelieving party would embrace the truth; but after his object is gained, he is further from the truth than before. And then begin the subtle workings, the continued efforts, of the enemy to draw away the believing one from the faith.

Many are now losing their interest and confidence in the truth because they have taken unbelief into close connection with themselves. They breathe the atmosphere of doubt, of questioning, of infidelity. They see and hear unbelief, and finally they cherish it. Some may have the courage to resist these influences, but in many cases their faith is imperceptibly undermined and finally destroyed.

Satan well knows that the hour that witnesses the marriage of many young men and women closes the history of their religious experience and usefulness. They are lost to Christ. They may for a time make an effort to live a Christian life, but all their strivings are made against a steady influence in the opposite direction. Once it was a privilege and joy to them to speak of their faith and hope, but they become unwilling to mention the subject, knowing that the one with whom they have linked their destiny takes no interest in it. As the result, faith in the precious truth dies out of the heart, and Satan insidiously weaves about them a web of skepticism.

The believing one reasons that in his new relation he must concede somewhat to the companion of his choice. Social, worldly amusements are patronized. At first there is great reluctance of feeling in doing this, but the interest in the truth becomes less and less, and faith is exchanged for doubt and unbelief.

What ought every Christian to do when brought into the trying position which tests the soundness of religious principle? With a firmness worthy of imitation he should say frankly, "I am a conscientious Christian. I believe the seventh day of the week to be the Sabbath of the Bible. Our faith and principles are such that they lead in opposite directions. We cannot be happy together, for if I follow on to gain a more perfect knowledge of the will of God, I shall become more and more unlike the world. If you continue to see no loveliness in Christ, no attractions in the truth, you will love the world, which I cannot love, while I shall love the things of God, which you cannot love.

You will not be happy; you will be jealous on account of the affections which I give to God; and I shall be alone in my religious belief. When your views shall change, when your heart shall respond to the claims of God, and you shall learn to love my Saviour, then our relationship may be renewed.

The believer thus makes a sacrifice for Christ which his conscience approves, and which shows that he values eternal life too highly to run the risk of losing it. He feels that it would be better to remain unmarried than to link his interest for life with one who chooses the world rather than Jesus.

Shall one who is seeking for glory, honor, immortality, eternal life, form a union with another who refuses to rank with the soldiers of the cross of Christ? Will you who profess to choose Christ for your master and to be obedient to Him in all things, unite your interests with one who is ruled by the prince of the powers of darkness? "Can two walk together, except they be agreed?"

Hundreds have sacrificed Christ and heaven in consequence of marrying unconverted persons. Can it be that love and fellowship of Christ are of so little value to them that they prefer the companionship of poor mortals.[3]

81

The letter to Rose deals with perhaps the most dangerous problem for young women—the question of marrying an unbeliever. This issue is certainly one of the most serious challenges to a happy Christian marriage.

The point that Ellen White considers with Rose is one that every girl might seriously think about—"listen to no promises." The issue of spiritual commitment is best settled *before* marriage, *not after*. As suggested in this letter—"it is a life or death question."

Dear Rose:

I have heard that you are intending to marry a man who is not a believer. I am unable to write you a long letter, but I will say if you take this step you depart from the plainest injunction of God's Word and cannot expect or claim His blessing upon such a union. All the promises of God are on condition of obedience to Him.

Satan stands ready to infatuate the mind and soul to pursue a course directly contrary to God's expressed will that he may separate that soul from God, and he interposes his temptations and obtains control over the mind and the heart's affections. This is Satan's studied plan to lead souls to turn from One mighty in counsel to the persuasion of minds who have no love for God, no love for the truth.

God has blessed you with great light and the Lord expects you to study His will, to carefully follow the directions given you in His Word. You are infatuated, you are being ensnared to your ruin. You have reason to be grateful to God every hour. Rely upon Him, whose wisdom is given in counsel in His holy Word. He has a care for His children above that of the most affectionate parent. He sees the end from the beginning, and for this reason has left us promises and cautions and has forbidden His children pursuing a certain course which will be ruinous to themselves.

The apostle Paul sends down the note of warning along the line to this time. ''Be ye not unequally yoked together with unbelievers: for what fellowship hath righteousness with unrighteousness? and what communion hath light with darkness? And what concord hath Christ with Belial? or what part hath he that believeth with an infidel? And what agreement hath the temple of God with idols? for ye are the temple of the living God; as God hath said, I will dwell in them, and walk in them; and I will be their God, and they shall be my people. Wherefore come out from among them, and be ye separate, saith the Lord, and touch not the unclean thing; and I will receive you, And will be a Father unto you, and ye shall be my sons and daughters, saith the Lord Almighty.'' (2 Cor. 6:14-18)

The Lord expressly has forbidden His people to marry with unbelievers. God knows what is best for the soul's eternal interest and for their present good. I warn you off from this forbidden ground.

I might tell you of different cases here that God has shown me in Europe who have made a similar mistake to that you are now making, the wretched reality they now experience of being bound to the unbelieving companions, hindered in all spiritual advancement, notwithstanding the solemn promises made that they would not in any way hinder them in their religious privileges. What are their promises worth? The most solemn promises broken! How can it be otherwise the two serving under different generals, one in deadly opposition to the other? Where, then, is the sweet harmony?

Rose, look well to your steps; listen to no promises, believe only the Word of God which will make you wise unto salvation. Trust not in your own heart for the heart is deceitful above all things and desperately wicked. I love your soul for you are the purchase of the blood of Jesus Christ. He has paid a dear price for your redemption, and you are not your own to dispose of yourself as you may think best. You must give a solemn account in the judgment how you have appropriated your God-given powers.

These things call for your serious reflection and decided action in accordance with the plainest directions laid down in the Word of God. Now is your time of temptation, now is your time of trial; will you resist the enemy? Or will you place yourself in a position where his power will be exercised over you?

It is a life or death question with you, May the Lord help you to see every snare of Satan and avoid it, and cling to Jesus with heart and soul and mind and strength.

Ellen G. White,

Letter 1, 1887

This letter to Laura looks at the question of marrying an unbeliever as did the previous one to Rose. Some rather pointed questions are asked by the prophet. How would you answer them if you were in Laura's place?

As you read this letter, other questions might well be asked of every girl who considers such a marriage. Are you being fair and honest with the young man who wants to marry you?

In this letter published in *Testimonies,* volume 5, Ellen White defines an unbeliever as one who "has not accepted the truth for this time."

St. Helena, Calif.
February 13, 1885

Dear Laura:

I have learned of your contemplated marriage with one who is not united with you in religious faith and I fear that you have not carefully weighed this important matter. Before taking a step which is to exert an influence upon all your future life, I urge you to give the subject careful and prayerful deliberation. Will this new relationship prove a source of true happiness? Will it be a help to you in the Christian life? Will it be pleasing to God? Will your example be a safe one for others to follow?

Before giving her hand in marriage, every woman should inquire whether he with whom she is about to unite her destiny is worthy. What has been his past record? Is his life pure? Is the love which he expresses of a noble, elevated character, or is it a mere emotional fondness? Has he the traits of character that will make her happy? Can she find true peace and joy in his affection? Will she be allowed to preserve her individuality, or must her judgment and conscience be surrendered to the control of her husband? As a disciple of Christ, she is not her own; she has been bought with a price. Can she honor the Saviour's claims as supreme? Will body and soul, thoughts and purposes, be preserved pure and holy? These questions have a vital bearing upon the well-being of every woman who enters the marriage relation.

Religion is needed in the home. Only this can prevent the grievous wrongs which so often embitter married life. Only where Christ reigns can there be deep, true, unselfish love. Angels of God will be guests in the home, and their holy vigils will hallow the marriage chamber.

I entreat you to ponder the step you contemplate taking. Ask yourself: "Will not an unbelieving husband lead my thoughts away from Jesus? He is a lover of pleasure more than a lover of God; will he not lead me to enjoy the things that he enjoys?" The path to eternal life is steep and rugged. Take no additional weights to retard your progress.

The Lord commanded ancient Israel not to intermarry with the idolatrous nations around them. The reason is given. Infinite Wisdom, foreseeing the result of such unions, declares: "For they will turn away thy son from following Me, that they may serve other gods: so will the anger of the Lord be kindled against you, and destroy thee suddenly." "For thou art an holy people unto the Lord thy God: the Lord thy God hath chosen thee to be a special people unto Himself, above all people that are upon the face of the earth."

In the New Testament are similar prohibitions concerning the marriage of Christians with the ungodly. "Be ye not unequally yoked together with unbelievers: for what fellowship hath righteousness with unrighteousness?"

Laura, dare you disregard these plain and positive directions? As a child of God a subject of Christ's kingdom, the purchase of His blood, how can you connect yourself with one who does not acknowledge His claims? who is not controlled by His Spirit? The commands I have quoted are not the word of man, but of God. Though the companion of your choice were in all other respects worthy (which he is not), yet he has not accepted the truth for this time; he is an unbeliever, and you are forbidden of heaven to unite yourself with him. You cannot, without peril to your soul, disregard this divine injunction.

You may say: "But I have given my promise, and shall I now retract it?" I answer: If you have made a promise contrary to the Scriptures, by all means retract it without delay, and in humility before God repent of the infatuation that led you to make so rash a pledge. Far better take back such a promise, in the fear of God, than keep it and thereby dishonor your Maker.

There is in the Christian world an astonishing, alarming indifference to the teaching of God's word in regard to the marriage of Christians with unbelievers. Many who profess to love and fear God choose to follow the bent of their own minds rather than take counsel of Infinite Wisdom. In a matter which vitally concerns the happiness and well-being of both parties for this world and the next, reason, judgment, and the fear of God are set aside, and blind impulse, stubborn determination, is allowed to control.

Men and women who are otherwise sensible and conscientious close their ears to counsel; they are deaf to the appeals and entreaties of friends and kindred and of the servants of God. The expression of a caution or warning is regarded as impertinent meddling, and the friend who is faithful enough to utter a remonstrance is treated as an enemy.

All this is as Satan would have it. He weaves his spell about the soul, and it becomes bewitched, infatuated. Reason lets fall the reins of self-control upon the neck of lust, unsanctified passion bears sway, until, too late, the victim awakens to a life of misery and bondage. This is not a picture drawn by the imagination, but a recital of facts. God's sanction is not given to unions which He has expressly forbidden.

For years I have been receiving letters from different persons who have formed unhappy marriages, and the revolting histories opened before me are enough to make the heart ache. It is no easy thing to decide what advice can be given to these unfortunate ones, or how their hard lot can be lightened; but their sad experience should be a warning to others.

You are under the most sacred obligation not to belittle or compromise your holy faith by uniting with the Lord's enemies. If you are tempted to disregard the injunctions of His word because others have done so, remember that your example also will exert an influence. Others will do as you do, and thus the evil will be extended.

The very strongest incentives to faithfulness are set before us, the highest motives, the most glorious rewards. Christians are to be Christ's representatives, sons and daughters of God.

May God help you to stand the test and preserve your integrity. Cling by faith to Jesus. Disappoint not your Redeemer.

With deepest affection,

Ellen G. White,

Letter in *Testimonies*, vol. 5, pp. 361-368

WILL YOU GAMBLE WITH YOUR MARRIAGE?

The unbelieving may possess an excellent moral character; but the fact that he or she has not answered to the claims of God, and has neglected so great salvation, is sufficient reason why such a union should not be consummated.

The plea is sometimes made that the unbeliever is favorable to religion and is all that could be desired in a companion except in one thing—he is not a Christian. Although the better judgment of the believer may suggest the impropriety of a union for life with an unbeliever, yet, in nine cases out of ten, inclination triumphs. Spiritual declension commences the moment the vow is made at the altar; religious fervor is dampened, and one stronghold after another is broken down, until both stand side by side under the black banner of Satan. Even in the festivities of the wedding, the spirit of the world triumphs against conscience, faith, and truth. In the new home the hour of prayer is not respected. The bride and bridegroom have chosen each other and dismissed Jesus.

At first the unbelieving one may make no show of opposition in the new relation; but when the subject of Bible truth is presented for attention and consideration, the feeling at once arises: "You married me, knowing that I was what I am; I do not wish to be disturbed. From henceforth let it be understood that conversation upon your peculiar views is to be interdicted!" If the believer should manifest any special earnestness in regard to his faith, it might seem like unkindness toward the one who has no interest in the Christian experience.[4]

Let those who are comtemplating marriage weigh every sentiment and watch every development of character in the one with whom they think to unite their life destiny. Let every step toward a marriage alliance be characterized by modesty, simplicity, sincerity, and an earnest purpose to please and honor God. Marriage affects the afterlife both in this world and in the world to come. A sincere Christian will make no plans that God cannot approve.[5]

James White and Ellen Harmon were married August 30, 1846. No wedding picture was taken at that time, but this picture taken in 1864 represented that occasion.

State of Maine.

Aug 31, 1846.

CUMBERLAND, ss.

THIS CERTIFIES, That Mr James L White

and Miss Ellen S. Hoomer of

Portland

were this day, joined in marriage, according to the laws of this

State, by me, *Charles Warden* Justice of the Peace.

John Edwards, Printer—Portland.

A reproduction of James and Ellen White's marriage license. The couple were married by a justice of the peace probably because, as believers in the second coming of Christ in the mid-1840s, they had been disfellowshiped from their churches. The Seventh-day Adventist Church, not organized until 1863, had no credentialed ministers when the White's married in 1846.

References

SECTION ONE

1. Patriarchs and Prophets, p. 46
2. Thoughts From the Mount of Blessing, pp. 63, 64
3. The Adventist Home, pp. 55, 56
4. The Ministry of Healing, pp. 357, 358
5. The Desire of Ages, p. 144
6. The Ministry of Healing, p. 356
7. The Adventist Home, p. 28
8. Thoughts From the Mount of Blessing, p. 64
9. The Ministry of Healing, p. 362
10. The Seventh-day Adventist Bible Commentary, vol. 5, p. 1140

SECTION TWO

1. The Ministry of Healing, p. 358
2. Education, p. 216
3. Testimonies, vol. 3, p. 156
4. The Ministry of Healing, p. 359
5. Testimonies, vol. 5, p. 362
6. Fundamentals of Christian Education, p. 105
7. The Ministry of Healing, p. 359

SECTION THREE

1. Testimonies, vol. 2, p. 248
2. Testimonies, vol. 5, pp. 122, 123
3. Review and Herald, Feb. 2, 1886
4. Patriarchs and Prophets, p. 176
5. Testimonies, vol. 2, p. 133
6. The Ministry of Healing, p. 358

7. *Testimonies,* vol. 2, pp. 134, 135

8. *Testimonies,* vol. 4, p. 548

9. *Review and Herald,* Feb. 2, 1886

10. *Testimonies,* vol. 2, pp. 135, 136

11. *Messages to Young People,* pp. 456-459

12. *Fundamentals of Christian Education,* p. 104

13. *Messages to Young People,* p. 438

SECTION FOUR

1. *The Desire of Ages,* p. 668

2. *The Adventist Home,* p. 43

3. *Messages to Young People,* p. 460

4. *Fundamentals of Christian Education,* p. 103

5. *The Adventist Home,* p. 70

6. *The Ministry of Healing,* p. 359

7. *Testimonies,* vol. 5, pp. 108, 109

8. *Fundamentals of Christian Education,* pp. 104-106

9. *Ibid.,* pp. 101, 102

SECTION FIVE

1. *Child Guidance,* p. 466

2. *Testimonies,* vol. 3, p. 84

3. *The Ministry of Healing,* p. 358

4. *Messages to Young People,* p. 452

5. *Fundamentals of Christian Education,* p. 105

6. *Acts of the Apostles,* p. 518

7. *The Adventist Home,* p. 404

8. *Ibid.,* pp. 127, 128

9. *Testimonies,* vol. 2, p. 410

10. *Review and Herald,* May 24, 1887

SECTION SIX

1. *Messages to Young People,* p. 30

2. *Ibid.,* p. 452

3. *Testimonies,* vol. 4, pp. 622, 623

4. *Medical Ministry,* pp. 142, 143

5. *Letter 18,* 1891

6. *The Seventh-day Adventist Bible Commentary,* vol. 2, p. 1032

7. *The Adventist Home,* p. 57

8. *Ibid.,* pp. 331, 332

9. *Testimonies,* vol. 5, pp. 596, 602

SECTION SEVEN

1. *Testimonies,* vol. 5, pp. 362-365

2. *Testimonies,* vol. 4, p. 507

3. *Ibid.,* pp. 504-507

4. *Ibid.,* pp. 505, 506

5. *The Ministry of Healing,* p. 359